WITHDRAWN

Copyright © 2011 by NordSüd Verlag AG, CH-8005 Zürich, Switzerland.
First published in Switzerland under the title *Filu im Schnee*.
English text copyright © 2011 by North-South Books Inc., New York 10001.
Translated by NordSüd Verlag. Edited by Susan Pearson.
All rights reserved.
No part of this book may be reproduced or utilized in any form or by any means,
electronic or mechanical, including photo-copying, recording, or any information
storage and retrieval system, without permission in writing from the publisher.

First published in the United States, Great Britain, Canada, Australia, and New Zealand in 2011
by North-South Books Inc., an imprint of NordSüd Verlag AG, CH-8005 Zürich, Switzerland.
Distributed in the United States by North-South Books Inc., New York 10001.

Library of Congress Cataloging-in-Publication Data is available.
Printed in Germany by Grafisches Centrum Cuno GmbH & Co. KG, 39240 Calbe, April 2011.
ISBN: 978-0-7358-4031-7 (trade edition)
1 3 5 7 9 • 10 8 6 4 2

www.northsouth.com

Meet Marcus Pfister at www.marcuspfister.ch.

FSC
www.fsc.org
MIX
Paper from
responsible sources
FSC® C043106

Marcus Pfister

Snow Puppy

NorthSouth
New York / London

Rascal was bored. Sophie had gone into the city to shop with her parents, but Rascal had to stay home all by himself. It was just plain mean. Rascal plopped his chin on his paws.

Then Rascal noticed something unusual outside the window. What was wrong with the sky? He jumped onto Dad's favorite chair and stood on his hind legs.

White specks were floating down from the sky. They looked just like those funny soft things that had swirled out of a pillow one time. Rascal had been playing with the pillow and torn it open. Then Sophie had chased after him, and Mom had chased after Sophie. It had been a lot of fun.

Rascal jumped off the chair and sped to the door. He had to jump up to the doorknob three times, but at last the door opened.

There was already a thick blanket of snow on the ground. Rascal raced around in it excitedly. The game with the snowflakes was as much fun as the game with the torn pillow. But the flakes were ice-cold, and when they landed on his nose they disappeared without a trace.

Something was moving near the fence! It was small
and brown, and now it was hopping across the field.
Rascal needed to get a closer look. Barking happily, he
leaped to the fence, squeezed through, and ran toward
the woods.

A new game! Rascal chased after the rabbit, farther and farther away from home. Suddenly the rabbit disappeared. It seemed as if it had been swallowed up by the ground. No matter how hard he tried, Rascal couldn't find it. He didn't give up, though. After all, he had a good nose. He sniffed and he sniffed until finally his nose led him to a mysterious hole. The rabbit must be hiding inside.

Rascal pushed his nose into the hole . . .
deeper . . . and deeper . . . until his head got stuck.
He kicked his legs to try to free himself.

The rabbit backed into the farthest corner of the hole.
It looked terrified. Rascal barked, but the more he tried
to reassure the rabbit with his friendly barks, the more
frightened the rabbit got.

Finally Rascal got his head free. He shook the dirt and snow from his fur. He wasn't so thrilled with the snow now. He was soaking wet and freezing cold—and he was hungry. He couldn't stop thinking about his food dish at home. But where *was* home? Rascal had no idea.

There was a delicious smell in the air—it smelled just like bologna. Rascal followed the scent to a clearing. There he found a man sitting on a log eating a bologna sandwich. Rascal cautiously approached.

"Come here, little dog. Don't be afraid," said the man in a deep friendly voice. "You look hungry." He tossed a piece of bologna to Rascal, who swallowed it in one bite.

"Come here," said the man again.

A person with a bologna sandwich couldn't be all that bad. Rascal jumped onto the man's lap and cuddled up under his coat.

"Poor thing," said the man. "You're shivering from the cold." He gave Rascal a bite of his sandwich. "Warm up. Then we'll go to town to sell my Christmas trees. It'll be nice to have a little help this year."

The man wrapped Rascal in a blanket and set
the pup beside him. Wow! Rascal had never been
on a horse-drawn sleigh. The mighty horse stomped
the ground impatiently.

"Giddyap, Martha!"

And they were off! Martha snorted in the cold
winter air, and the heavy sleigh slid through the white
countryside. The clanging of Martha's bells and the
rocking of the sleigh lulled Rascal softly to sleep.

"We're there, my little friend," said the man, waking Rascal from his sleep. The man unloaded the pine trees from his sleigh. Thousands of Christmas lights lit up the square. The marketplace hustled and bustled with shoppers. Rascal watched shyly from his cozy blanket. He missed Sophie and his nice warm home.

Suddenly Rascal heard a familiar voice. "Daddy, look! This little tree is beautiful!"

Rascal leaped from the sleigh barking, and sprang into Sophie's arms.

"Rascal, what are *you* doing here?" cried Sophie.

The man explained how he had found Rascal in the woods.

"We can't thank you enough," said Mom. "It would have been a sad Christmas without Rascal!"

Then Mom invited the man to come for Christmas dinner.

"That's very kind of you," said the man. "But I couldn't possibly accept."

At that, Rascal snatched the corner of the man's coat and pulled with all his might.

"Well, I guess I have no choice," said the man, laughing.

Rascal wagged his tail in agreement, and the whole family looked forward to a very special Christmas.